What Do They Make?

by Mary Louise Bourget
illustrated by Bill Ogden

Harcourt

Orlando   Boston   Dallas   Chicago   San Diego

Visit *The Learning Site!*

www.harcourtschool.com

What do they make?

 They make a bike.

It is little.

 They make a seesaw.

It is little.

They make a car.

It is big!